"Herman, you can get in the bathroom now"

Other Herman Books

The 1st Treasury of Herman
The Second Herman Treasury
Herman, The Third Treasury
Herman: The Fourth Treasury
Herman Treasury 5
Herman, The Sixth Treasury
Herman Over the Wall: The Seventh Treasury
"Herman, Dinner's Served ...
as Soon as the Smoke Clears!"
Herman, You Were a Much Stronger Man
on Our First Honeymoon
The Latest Herman
"They're Gonna Settle Out of Court, Herman"

"Herman, you can get in the bathroom now"

by Jim Unger

Andrews and McMeel
A Universal Press Syndicate Company
Kansas City • New York

HERMAN® is syndicated internationally by
Universal Press Syndicate.

"Herman, you can get in the bathroom now"
copyright © 1987 by Universal Press Syndicate. All
rights reserved. Printed in the United States of
America. No part of this book may be used or
reproduced in any manner whatsoever without
written permission except in the case of reprints
in the context of reviews. For information write
Andrews and McMeel, a Universal Press Syndicate
Company, 4900 Main Street, Kansas City, Missouri
64112.

ISBN: 0-8362-2094-3

Library of Congress Catalog Card Number: 87-71452

First Printing, July 1987
Seventh Printing, March 1991

"Mother, I wish you wouldn't rent those old disco movies."

"How's the water?"

"When are you people going to get that elevator fixed?"

"Yes, we know what it is. We want to know where you got it!"

"He was on a one-day strike at work today and nobody noticed."

"Couldn't you hear that phone ringing?"

"Is this the fifty-four-year-old limbo dancer?"

"I told you we should have had the driveway paved."

8

"I thought you were going to mow the lawn."

"Why don't you leave the ring and
I'll phone you with my answer."

"Listen, I'd better go. My wife's waiting to use the phone."

"I'm here on a student exchange program."

"He's trying to hatch some duck eggs."

"There's just no pleasing you, is there?
All week you've been telling me to get a haircut."

"I didn't have the time to get you any flowers."

"I'm not going to give you a tip. I
don't like to hurt people's feelings."

"He painted this one while
he was locked in his studio."

"I want my apple back."

13

"Luckily, our honeymoon suite had a TV in the bedroom."

"I told you not to drink that on an empty stomach."

"Same as yesterday: one sausage,
four french fries, and eleven peas."

"Stick your tongue out. I want to clean my glasses."

"I always wear my lucky hat for job interviews."

"Two round-the-world cruises in opposite directions."

16

"Are you gonna be able to afford a car
by the time I need to borrow it?"

"Just put it back on the wall."

"We're going to Italy for a
week on his overtime pay."

"I thought you *liked* shepherd's pie!"

"I usually have to drive him home after a party."

"I was rubbing two sticks together
and discovered first-degree burns."

"I need 148 get-well cards."

"I can't bring the car back 'til low tide."

"Four blocks north. If it's
not there, eight blocks south."

"I rolled the car on the way to band practice."

"I know there's a full moon tonight.
Don't keep thinking about it."

"You've got exactly fifteen seconds to start
putting up that wallpaper in our bedroom."

"I'm not worried about *his* future. We were only in the park ten minutes."

"How many times have I told you not to call me at work?"

23

"Can't you make less noise when you eat?"

"You put the comics page in here.
You know he likes the editorials."

"Will you *please* ask your mother
to sit over on my side?"

"Don't creep around. I heard the
garage door three minutes ago."

25

"Your doctor wants to marry
me if you don't make it."

"Don't keep saying, 'I wonder what it tastes like'!"

"Now that you've cut off my electricity, how do you expect me to find my checkbook in the dark?"

"I hit it with the truck."

"OK, you can stop signaling now."

"Today's special is all the caviar you can eat for $600."

"She can say 'charge it' in fourteen languages."

"I think I'll give it a shot on my own today, Bernie."

"Fifteen seconds away from a peaceful night."

"Did you lock the *back* door?"

"Vertical stripes definitely make you look slimmer."

"I know the tablecloth's dirty. Don't forget
this place has been open since 1963."

"How many times have I told you
not to starch my shirts?"

"Your boss wants to hear you cough."

"He makes $35 an hour as an electrician."

"The airline lost my luggage again."

"Pull up to the front of that apartment building and leave the engine running."

"They haven't built the crib that can hold me."

"I've got to get some new curtains for the living
room. Where did you hide the $6 million?"

"If you order the chili, I need
to know your next-of-kin."

"Open this up exactly halfway between
Christmas and your birthday."

"That's the big clock in the kitchen."

"Don't ask."

"Don't mess around. I know where you are."

"O'Reilly, did you leave this junk on my desk?"

"He's got his grandfather's nose."

"To be honest, I'd heard you'd gone abroad."

"You're being released. Be ready
to leave in thirty minutes."

40

"Keep your mouth closed when you're eating."

"You just plug it in once a month."

"I wouldn't be able to see a thing if
she hadn't had her ears pierced."

"Listen, I've got to go. That guy's still hanging
around waiting to use the phone."

"He moved!"

"I'll have two eggs and some b-a-c-o-n."

"Did you advertise for an experienced
salesman in ladies underwear?"

"He fell off the corporate ladder when
he asked for the minimum wage."

44

"How could *anyone* flush a goldfish down a sink?!"

"So then I said, 'The turning point in the women's liberation movement came when some guy invented the automatic transmission.'"

"You don't get atmosphere like
this watching it on television."

"I bought the first cup last Tuesday."

"I did quite a bit of painting in the hospital."

"Don't use that thing, I'll get the spray."

"Every time you take him for a walk he gets longer!"

"He's been at the video rental store all afternoon, doctor."

"She needs wider skis."

"Nurse!"

49

"Okay, rinse."

"You're not getting enough vitamin C."

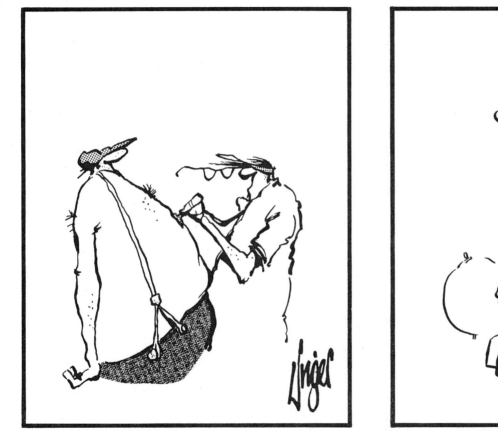

"Breathe out."

"What is he ever going to need to know about algebra? Stick to this country."

"Her idea of a balanced diet is four pounds of
chocolate with four pounds of cake."

"Couldn't he wait?"

52

"I'm waiting to hear you wipe your feet!"

"I've put a towel for your mother in here and
I'll use the bathroom downstairs."

"Good evening. I'm Andre, your Heimlich Maneuver specialist."

"I don't need anything, dear. I'll stay in bed until the fever dies down."

"Don't *nag*. If you want the light out, say so!"

"Non-smoking, unless you're expecting turbulence."

"This guy wants to know if we deliver to Africa."

"I usually leave an extra $10
in my pocket on her birthday."

"Your wife says you stopped a runaway horse."

"The tow truck will be an hour.
Why don't we rotate the tires?"

"This is my rent check. Make sure it circles the globe a few times."

"My husband will be doing all the parking."

"I told you not to order a Zombie in here."

"Hold it! Hold it! My whole life
is flashing before my eyes."

"It's nothing to worry about. You just need to drink more water."

"Read the instructions very, very, very, very carefully."

"There's a $100 bill in here!"

"None of those buildings used to be there."

"Does that hurt?"

"How can you tell if an uncut diamond is genuine?"

62

"Don't forget to take out the garbage."

"I caught it in a copier machine."

"The elephant fainted and we can't find the keeper."

"Will you please take this thing away from him. I'm *trying* to read."

"I am well aware that it's a religious holiday. But you can't deduct Christmas expenses from your taxes."

"You know Christmas is the only chance Daddy gets to sleep in!"

"Guess which tree my dad hit."

"Rambo ... Robert ... Michael."

"You left this refrigerator open again."

"There's a girl here who's been left $100 million! Why don't you give her a call?"

"You've heard of 'The Battle of the Bulge.' Well, you lost."

"He asked me to put some ketchup in here."

"Well, I just hope I look as good as you do on *my* 110th birthday."

"Nervous flier. ... He promised me an extra ten bucks if I miss his plane."

"Who's having the raw herring?"

"I'm outside the railway station after three o'clock."

"The *other* scraper!"

ENGLISH LITERATURE

"Shakespeare, did your father
help you with this homework?"

"I thought you liked this perfume!"

"She never wants to go out."

"Hey, Harry, can I have the key to the sugar?"

"What time did he discharge himself?"

"You don't want us to become extinct, do you?"

"Don't keep ducking."

"Doctor, I'm not getting a pulse."

"He told me to wake him at *exactly* eight o'clock."

"Good luck, Miller. Try to stay out of trouble."

"Try to remember all the things you've eaten in the past three days."

"Chest, fifteen and three-quarters."

"You know better than to make
a bed like *that*, nurse."

77

"Who's next?"

"Five cans of ceiling white."

"Sure, come over to dinner one evening. You can have mine."

"D'you want 'Outpatients' or 'Emergency'?"

"Come along, dear. Daddy's not supposed to go home today."

"It's for you, Mildred."

"For crying out loud ... it's a mirror!"

"They're gonna use your X-rays in a textbook!"

"Is that supposed to be a tip?"

"I love you too, sweetheart, but I've gotta go."

"Now don't you start that sales resistance
stuff — I've had a rough day."

"We'd love to have you over for dinner,
but we only have nine chairs."

"They warned us in hairdressing college this day would come."

"You guys are too early ... he's not in here yet."

"Got anything for vine-burn?"

"Who am I? And what am I doing here?"

"Just follow the blue line until
you find your insurance card."

"You've had a triple bypass."

"Oh, no! Right over the old ladies home!"

"You'll strain your eyes looking for a job that close!"

"His doctor told him to get some mountain air."

"Did you ask about getting me a bigger room?"

"It *is* an emergency! The potatoes are burning my head."

"OK, let's start from where I told you I needed a man who could use his head."

"Don't keep shouting 'call the plumber.' I've called the plumber."

"I'm not break-dancing! I hit my hand."

"So you were three days into the
mountains, then what happened?"

"Can we discuss salary first?
My wife's waiting to go shopping."

"Don't bother to leave a tip.
I had one of your sausages."

"I take it we're turning right."

"I'm the dishwasher out back.
Hide my tip in the gravy."

"They found your other ski."

93

"Nurse, can we get some chairs over here?!"

"You can have that three-legged one for $7.50."

"It must be your pronunciation. Let me try."

"We've got to wait for the shock to wear off.
He nearly drove off an 800-foot cliff."

"What do you mean you overslept? That's the
third battle you missed this month!"

"Did your mother say you could
build a nuclear device?"

"Two years is a long time to have jet lag."

"You shouldn't carry all this cash.
Why don't you open an account?"

"I told you never to get between
Mother and a dessert trolley."

"It's $500, but that includes a
month's supply of breath mints."

"Good news and bad news. The good news is he won't be scratching your furniture anymore."

"Just because it's your turn to change his diaper!"

"Ask him where he left his
key to the safe-deposit box"

"You're supposed to let wine breathe."

100

"Don't kill it! It'll fly away on its own."

"If you can spare five seconds,
I'd like to do a brain scan."

"In time of war, they could drop you
behind enemy lines with that frying pan."

"I've gotta get a sample of your stomach acid."

"If you're *that* worried about catching it, sleep in the stupid kitchen."

"I've been elected to the Credit Card Hall of Fame."

"Whaddyer mean 'the oil's only lukewarm'?
They'll be attacking in ten minutes!"